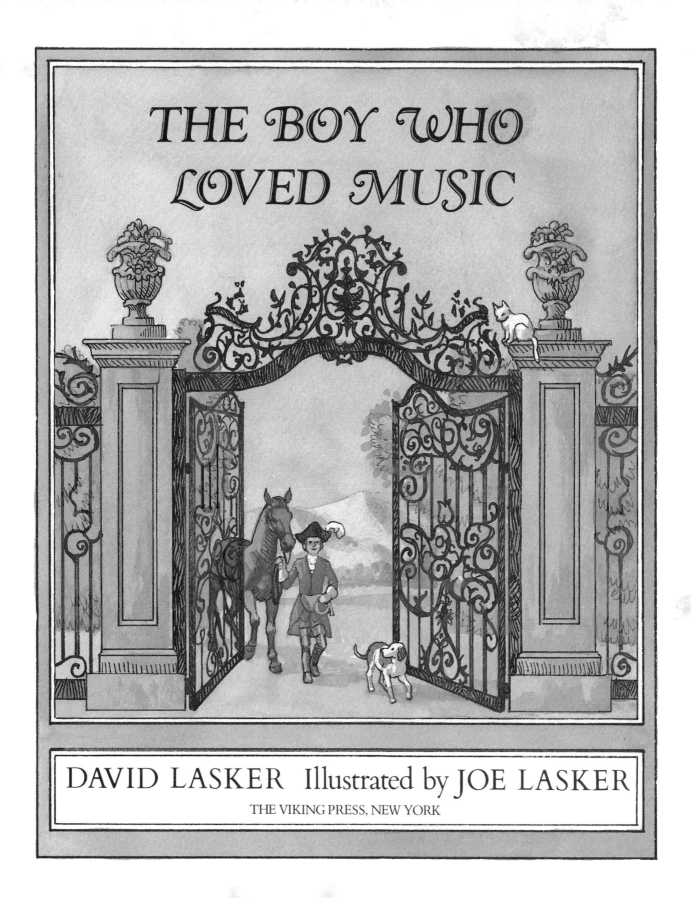

THE BOY WHO
LOVED MUSIC

DAVID LASKER   Illustrated by JOE LASKER

THE VIKING PRESS, NEW YORK

For Cam

D.L.

Text Copyright © David Lasker, 1979
Illustrations Copyright © Joe Lasker, 1979
All rights reserved. First published in 1979 by The Viking Press,
625 Madison Avenue, New York, N.Y. 10022. Published simultaneously
in Canada by Penguin Books Canada Limited. Printed in U.S.A.
2   3   4   5   83   82   81

Library of Congress Cataloging in Publication Data
Lasker, David. The boy who loved music.
Summary: To amuse the stubborn Prince Nicolaus Esterhazy,
who refuses to allow the court musicians to return to Vienna
at summer's end, Joseph Haydn composes a special "Farewell" symphony.
1. Haydn, Joseph, 1732-1809—Juvenile literature. [1. Haydn, Joseph, 1732-1809.
2. Composers] I. Lasker, Joe. II. Title.
ML3930.H3L4   780'.92'4 [B]   [92]   79-14651   ISBN 0-670-18385-7

Music was the main source of entertainment in the eighteenth century. A musician was a wealthy nobleman's servant, and his life was no better than that of the lord's cook, maid, or stableboy. Neither a slave nor a free man, the musician had to wait for his lord's permission if he wanted to travel, visit his family, or get married. If he grew impatient and didn't wait, the lord could throw him into jail.

This is the story of Karl, a young horn player, and his life in the great European castle of Esterhaza. It is based on historical fact, the composition of Haydn's "Farewell" Symphony, in 1772.

KARL

$Prince\ Nicolaus\ Esterhazy,$ the richest nobleman in Hungary, owned millions of acres and dozens of castles. The largest was Esterhaza, the most magnificent castle in the Austrian Empire. The Prince was so fond of it that, even though it was a summer palace, he stayed there later and later each

year. Summer ended and autumn began, yet the Prince would not return to Vienna, capital city of the Empire.

And while the Prince stayed, Esterhaza's musicians, singers, actors, dancers, and painters stayed too. They were lonely; the Prince forbade them to visit their families except during those few months when he returned to his winter palace.

Joseph Haydn, the famous composer, was the music director at Esterhaza. At a rehearsal one day in October 1772 he spoke to his musicians. "Gentlemen," he said, tapping his violin bow against his music stand, "I know you are all tired and homesick. This season our lord has kept us here longer than ever before. But you know why: the Empress Maria Theresa will visit Esterhaza for a few days and we must make a good impression. When she returns to Vienna, Prince Nicolaus will surely follow, and of course we will go with him. Now, let us tune our instruments and begin the rehearsal."

Tomasini, the principal violinist, bounced his bow on the strings as he practiced some difficult music. "How do they expect me to read these notes?" he complained to himself. "They look like ink blots! The copyist ought to have his paw chopped off."

Xavier, the bass viol player, was a tall man, but his instrument was taller. He winced as he twisted the tuning pegs. The long strings were stretched so tightly that the pegs always slipped loose. He took longer to tune than anyone else, and the other musicians liked to joke about it.

"I'll bet you wish you played the piccolo," teased Karl, the young horn player.

Xavier was irritated. "I've heard that one before, Karl, at least a thousand times," he said.

Suddenly cannons fired in the distance.

"The Empress! The Empress is arriving!" said Haydn. "No time to re-hearse now. Quick, gentlemen, to the gateway."

The musicians took their instruments and rushed to a flower-decked platform that faced the gateway to the Vienna road. Prince Nicolaus, in a golden sedan chair carried by footmen, held a lace handkerchief in his right hand.

When he saw the Empress's party approach, he waved the handkerchief in the air. The great spectacle began.

The trumpets and drums played a rousing "ta-ran-ta-ra," and one hundred and fifty grenadiers fired their muskets into the sky. Serfs from the villages around Esterhaza crowded both sides of the road and cheered.

The royal coach stopped at the gate. It bore the coat of arms of the Hapsburgs, Europe's mightiest royal family for five hundred years. Out stepped Her Imperial Majesty, the Empress Maria Theresa. Her jewel-laden hoopskirt was so wide that she had to turn sideways to squeeze through the doorway of her coach.

The Prince led his guests to the palace, where they refreshed themselves; later he entertained them with an opera. The musicians, led by Haydn, were sandwiched between the audience and the singers on the stage.

As they played, they thought, Each note brings us closer to the end of an-other day. Each note brings us closer to Vienna and to our families and friends.

After the opera the royal guests visited a country fair in a nearby village, where thousands of peasants in colorful costumes swarmed through the streets. One group danced gypsy dances, another sang folk songs, while some tugged hungrily at breads and sausages that hung from the trees.

There were many sideshows. A dentist strutted about on twenty-foot-high stilts, brandishing a pair of gigantic tooth-pulling pliers. A company of traveling clowns batted one another with enormous clubs. Their wagon was pulled by tigers and monkeys.

"How funny," Karl said to Xavier as they wandered through the crowds, "that Prince Nicolaus should assemble these curiosities for the amusement of his guests. He doesn't realize how strange his guests appear to us!"

Xavier agreed. The noblemen, following the Prince's example, competed

for the most expensive, most outlandish clothing, while each lady wanted her hair arrangement to be the most eye-catching. One countess's hair had been glued up till it was two feet tall; it was topped with a bird's nest. It was said she had slept all night propped up in a chair. "Not much of a sacrifice to appear in the height of fashion!" said Karl with a smile.

"Step right up and see Maria Theresa's gallant soldiers conquer the enemy," shouted the owner of the peep show. This portable box enclosed a series of pictures of a battle that could be viewed through a small opening. Everyone laughed. When foreign noblemen from different countries visited Esterhaza, the peep

show's owner told them that they were viewing their *own* gallant soldiers. The names of the countries changed, but the peep show was always the same. The noblemen never knew.

In the evening there was a masked ball, a popular form of entertainment for the nobility.

Confident that they could not be recognized underneath their costumes, they flirted with one another and had a good time.

The following morning a servant rudely shook Karl awake. "Get up," he said. "The Prince wants to go on a fox hunt."

"I wish I were home in Vienna instead of chasing a silly fox," Karl said sleepily.

"Don't argue with the Prince's orders," said the servant as he left. Karl cursed the Prince for staying at Esterhaza so late into the autumn. He cursed himself for being a horn player.

Most women, who by custom could only ride side-saddle, stayed behind. Some women played croquet while others bathed, but it took so long to fill a bathtub that none of them—or their noblemen, either—washed more often than once a month. The servants bathed about once a year.

Prince Nicolaus had set aside thousands of acres of woods as his private hunting preserve. Pity the countryman who dared to enter it to hunt for himself! Prince Nicolaus had no mercy.

Karl was the huntmaster who rode at the head of the pack as it charged out of the castle grounds. He was needed, not to make music, but to blow loud

horn calls to the hounds, which were trained to respond to the sound. One call signaled them to start running after the fox's scent. If the animal turned out to be a vixen with young pups, Prince Nicolaus wanted her set free, so Karl would blow another call that would stop the hounds from killing her.

Karl used a small horn for hunting, which, unlike his larger orchestral horn, could sound only a few notes. Like many horn players of his time, he was always afraid that someday his horse would lunge forward, bang the mouthpiece against his teeth, and knock them out. If that happened, he would never be able to play the horn again.

On this hunt the terrified fox tried to escape by running out of the forest and into a nearby village. The hunters followed and trampled several peasant gardens and nearly ran down some children. But they galloped on.

Afterward Karl rushed to join the others at lunch. He was dusty, sweaty, and out of breath. Xavier called out, "I'll bet you wish you played the bass." Everyone laughed, but Karl was angry.

"It's not fair!" he yelled, stamping his feet. "Prince Nicolaus has no right to keep us here this long!" The laughing stopped. Everyone felt as Karl did. "It's late October," said Xavier. "I haven't seen my family for seven months."

"Alas," Haydn sighed, "just look at this leathery old chunk of cow! Try eating these miserable apple fritters!"

Karl sat down and looked out the window. Toward the west was Vienna, where he'd played horn duets with his father and sung songs with his sisters and mother. "Oh," he said, "I wish I could say farewell to this place."

The Empress departed, and only a few guests remained. After the days of intense activity Esterhaza was quiet. A week passed, then two weeks. The days

grew shorter and colder; the leaves dropped off the trees, but Prince Nicolaus was still at Esterhaza.

At last Haydn spoke to the Prince. He walked into the audience chamber and bowed deeply. "Exalted and illustrious Prince, I kiss your noble hands. I beg you to receive this plea: when would it please Your Majesty to depart?"

The Prince, himself a musician, was fond of Haydn. When Haydn's house in Vienna had burned down, Prince Nicolaus had immediately built him a larger one. He had never before kept his musicians away for so long; he knew how they felt. But to leave his beloved Esterhaza now? The peaceful gardens? The splashing fountains? He dabbed his nostrils with a pinch of snuff and said quietly, "Haydn may tell our musicians that we shall depart Esterhaza when we desire it."

Haydn responded in the formal manner that was expected of him. "Gracious and dread lord and sire, I thank you for your infinite kindness. I remain now and my whole life your most humble and obedient servant."

Karl met Haydn after the audience and asked if the Prince was ready to leave. "Ready? I'm afraid we'll never get out of here."

Then Karl noticed Baron von Scheffstoss, the Prince's secretary, at the head of the grand staircase. On an impulse Karl ran up the marble steps.

"Honorable Baron, please ask the Prince to let us go home," Karl said breathlessly.

The Baron became stiff as a statue and red with rage. "How dare you!" he thundered. "Who do you think you are, you lowborn riffraff! I'll have you thrown into the dungeon! Now get out!" With that, he jabbed Karl, who stumbled backward down the stairs.

Haydn, trying not to laugh, helped Karl up. "You young hothead! Don't you know better than to approach a nobleman like that?"

Karl brushed himself off. "Just trying to help," he said.

"That's not the way, Karl. Prince Nicolaus won't be won over by rudeness. We've got to do something that will amuse him. He'd like that."

"If all the musicians got up in the middle of your next performance and marched off to Vienna, *I'd* be amused."

"Hmm. That's not bad! I like your idea, Karl. Let's give it a try."

A few days later the orchestra performed for Prince Nicolaus and his few
remaining guests.

They played the symphony Haydn had just composed. It had a surprise ending.

Karl played a solo; then, while the others went on playing, he blew out the candles alongside his music stand, packed up his horn under his arm, and

walked off into the side room. Xavier did the same and lugged off his heavy bass viol. They waited by the door and watched the Prince's astonished face.

One by one, the musicians left. Only a few violinists and cellists remained. The sound of this small group was much softer than that of the full orchestra. A great stillness settled over the room, a sighing, wistful sadness. The music told the Prince how the musicians felt: homesick and lonely.

More players departed. Only Haydn and Tomasini remained. Finally they, too, put out their candles and withdrew. The symphony was over. Prince Nicolaus stood up. "What an ingenious symphony! Congratulations, Haydn," he said. Then he turned to his guests and announced, "If they all leave, we may as well leave, too."

"Bravo! Hooray for Haydn!" the musicians cheered, shaking hands and slapping backs. Xavier and Tomasini hoisted Haydn onto their shoulders.

Karl blew a loud horn call and they marched triumphantly back to their quarters.

They all left for Vienna the next day.

DATE DUE
